A Conservation Tale

The Three Little Lemurs

AARON GROPE

Book and cover design by Patricia Bacall
Illustrations by Julia Morga and Aaron Grope

Do You Love Lemurs?
I Love Lemurs...

...and I wrote this book to help save lemurs from extinction. If we understand the story of lemurs—their origins, diversity and how they exist in their unique environment—we will better understand humanity and how it came to be. If we lose lemurs, we lose part of our own story. I give my deepest thanks to Tammy Falcone who helped me to understand that all stories are possible, and to my mom who taught me that we should always dream big enough to make a positive change in the world.

—Aaron Grope, 2020

This is an adaptation of the famous folktale, "Three Little Pigs". It takes place on the island of Madagascar, and the "pigs" are not pigs at all, they're LEMURS! (pronounced Lee-Murz). The purpose of this book is to create awareness about lemurs; in particular the ring-tailed lemur, their habitat, and the dangers that are threatening them.

3

5 Quick Facts Before You Read

1. MADAGASCAR! Lemurs are members of the primate (monkey) family, that can only be found living on the fourth largest island in the world, Madagascar. They are believed to have "floated" to Madagascar on chunks of land-like-rafts millions of years ago. Since Madagascar has been separated from the rest of the world for some 150 million years, the lemurs evolved and adapted into over thirty species that fit into each of the island's unique habitats.

2. DRY DRY DRY! Ring-tailed lemurs live in the dry woodlands off the southeastern coast. Their favorite food is the fruit pods from the Kily tree, also known as Tamarind. They also eat leaves, flowers, bark, sap, and bugs. Because it is so dry, their water comes from plants, dew, and sips from rivers when they can find them.

3. HIP HOP! Almost 40% of the Ring-tailed Lemurs time is spent on the ground. Their long, black and white striped tail helps them balance when they leap, run, and dance-hop along. They also "wave" their tails like a flag to keep their family group together, acting as a tour guide. Unlike most other primates, their tail is not used for hanging or swinging.

4. LEMURS ARE NOISY and SMELLY! They "talk" to one another not only with their facial expressions, but with over fifteen sounds like grunts, clicks, screeches, howls, and purrs. They also use the scent glands on their wrists and tails to leave smelly sticky notes to each other to mark their territory and keep family troops together.

5. ENDANGERED! Ring-tailed lemurs are endangered, mostly because their dry forests are disappearing. Forests are often burned to clear land for cattle, plant crops, or to make charcoal for cooking. Tavy is the process the locals use to cut down trees and burn the logs, otherwise known as slash and burn. Humans' pets like cats and dogs, as well as natural predators like hawks and fossas, which are cat-like relatives of the mongoose, hunt the lemurs as well.

6

Once upon a time, just off the dry, southeastern coast of Africa, three little lemurs were lazing about. Sitting crosslegged lotus-style, they soaked up the sun with their arms, legs, and bellies outstretched to warm up after a chilly night. This was their routine before beginning to forage for that day's snack. Their home island was just right for them and 100-200 other species of lemurs... "cousins" you might say. Sunbathing was just great until they all got hungry and decided to head off on their own to find themselves a snack. They all went to their special places in the rain forest to gather their favorite treats.

The first little lemur leaped hungrily from limb to limb, way up high, near the sky where every lemur knows the best fruit grows.

8

"Mmm!" chirped and howled the first little lemur, as he bit into his favorite sour-tasting fruit pod of the Kily tree. "This is the perfect spot to stay for a while," and he settled in to nibble.

9

Little did the first little lemur know that a Big Bad Fire had just been released by humans from its captivity in a matchbox. It moved like a fossa, devouring the trees in its path, splitting and growing new hungry mouths at every turn.

The fire roared, "Little lemur, Little lemur, let me have your Kily tree!"

11

"Not by the hair of my long hairy tail! My forest will always be free!" barked the first little lemur. Little lemur lept just in the nick of time, launching himself off through the brush to find his two brothers.

The Big Bad Fire followed along behind.

13

eanwhile, the second little lemur strolled along the forest floor on all fours, pausing to dance a little jig when he found a fallen mango fruit to feast upon. "Oooh, this is my lucky day!" mewed and purred the second little lemur. *As* he settled into munch, sweet liquid-sunshine dribbled down his long, pointed nose.

Sniff Sssnufff Ssnniff...

"Uh oh! I smell smoke! That means danger to my forest!"

The second little lemur wailed his alarm, OOOoooWWoAAhhaaha!" If his brothers were within a ten-mile radius, they would hear him and come running.

17

Just then, along came the Big Bad Fire, hang-gliding through the treetops like a hungry Harrier hawk.

The fire roared, "Little lemur! Little lemur! Let me have your mango tree!"

"Not by the hair of my long hairy tail! My forest will always be free!"

19

The second little lemur lept away from the fire just in the nick of time, launching himself off through a maze of vines. The very same nose that had sensed danger led him to follow the trail of his first brothers' scent.

As soon as they saw each other, they went in search of their third brother.

21

Meanwhile, after having scarfed down a couple of leaves, flowers, AND a fig for a snack, the third little lemur headed downward to sip water from the river. It was his tail, standing straight up, waving like a striped flag that caught his brothers' attention. Their chirps of happiness echoed through the forest, but only for a second.

24

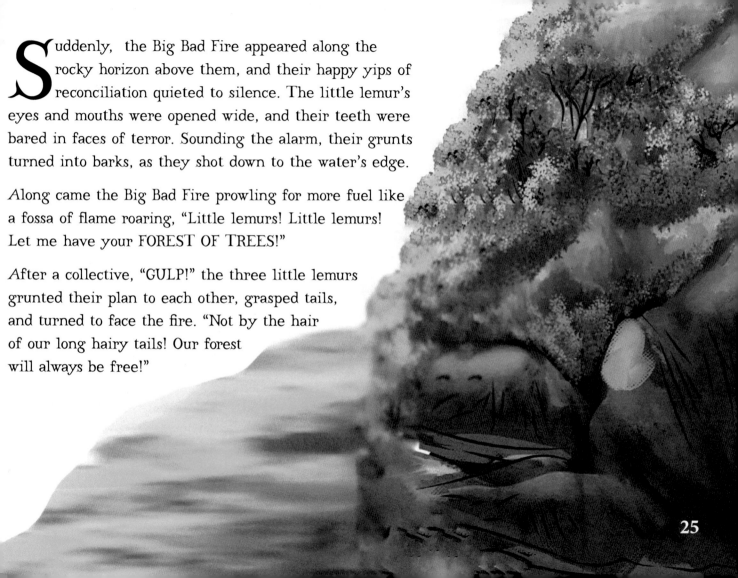

Suddenly, the Big Bad Fire appeared along the rocky horizon above them, and their happy yips of reconciliation quieted to silence. The little lemur's eyes and mouths were opened wide, and their teeth were bared in faces of terror. Sounding the alarm, their grunts turned into barks, as they shot down to the water's edge.

Along came the Big Bad Fire prowling for more fuel like a fossa of flame roaring, "Little lemurs! Little lemurs! Let me have your FOREST OF TREES!"

After a collective, "GULP!" the three little lemurs grunted their plan to each other, grasped tails, and turned to face the fire. "Not by the hair of our long hairy tails! Our forest will always be free!"

25

The three little lemurs slyly taunted, "Big Bad fire, if you want our forest, come on down and take it!"

Shooting down the ravine, the sleek, starving fire lept torwards the opposite bank of the river where there was a large stand of Kili trees. The fire went so fast, it didn't notice the shimmering water in it's path. It ran SMACK into the river.

Pffffsssssssssss....hissed the fire, as it fizzled and died.

26

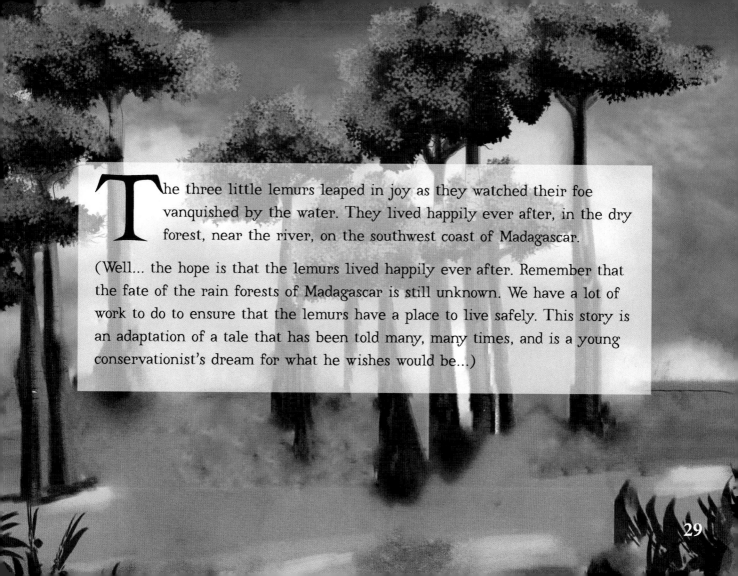

The three little lemurs leaped in joy as they watched their foe vanquished by the water. They lived happily ever after, in the dry forest, near the river, on the southwest coast of Madagascar.

(Well... the hope is that the lemurs lived happily ever after. Remember that the fate of the rain forests of Madagascar is still unknown. We have a lot of work to do to ensure that the lemurs have a place to live safely. This story is an adaptation of a tale that has been told many, many times, and is a young conservationist's dream for what he wishes would be...)

ABOUT THE AUTHOR

Aaron Grope is currently twelve years old and lives with his mother, father and two brothers in Greenwood Village, Colorado. His passion for lemurs started when he was only three years old and he began collecting them wherever he went. His interest was really sparked when his family took him to see the Imax movie "Island of Lemurs" at the Denver Museum of Nature and Science at the age of five. His passion has been studying lemurs ever since and has expanded to include conservation issues across the globe.

Aaron's goal is to help create awareness about lemurs and the need to preserve them in their natural habitat of Madagascar.

DO YOU WANT TO HELP THE LEMURS?

What you can do if you have...

10 minutes	1 hour	1 month	$100.00
• Learn about Lemurs and how to help them by reading a picture book like mine.	• Watch *Island of Lemurs: Madagascar* – a documentary that follows Patricia Wright's mission to help Lemurs.	• Volunteer for lemur conservation network as a blogger, designer, or illustrator.	• Consider symbolically adopting a Lemur or make a direct donation at defenders.org.
• Check out defenders.org for ideas on how you can help Lemurs.	• Visit your local zoo's lemurs. Watch. Look. Listen.	• Volunteer for Rescue Center Lemur rehabilitation.	• Help fund a fire prevention documentary, visit http://www.planetmadagascar.com/
• Check out lemurconservation.org.	• Visit Wildlife Action center at defenders.org and write a message to government leaders.		• Donate to plant trees and reforest Madagascar for as little as $0.10 per tree.
• Read *Scholastic News*.			• http://www.edenprojects.org/madagascar
			• Make a donation to the Duke Lemur Center at lemur.duke.edu

Thanks for reading!

I hope that you have learned about lemurs and their plight for survival in Madagascar. I also hope that you have learned about their life and how beautiful Madagascar is!

Join me on social media to learn the latest on what I'm doing to help the lemurs.

Facebook: Save all the Lemurs

Instagram: @saveallthelemurs

Email: saveallthelemurs@gmail.com

All proceeds from the sale of this book will be donated to organizations that help conservation efforts in Madagascar.